abandoned muse

Khayan Jefferson

To everyone who told me to pack it up, thank you.

The path of forgetting is forged by the one who is forced to remember it all

☽ ○☾

it is me who dreams of delusion

peach rings, candy dreams

what can you see in the stars, really?

food for thought

find love for the art, find a love for the artist

i've missed how you taste in my imagination

my heart moves faster than my reality can check it

a spiritual wake-up call for an emotional coma

salt and vinegar

i'm missing a tooth, i'm missing you

the burden of remembering

regretful obsession

abandon your muses, it's for the better

it is me who dreams of delusion
❧ ❧ ❧

I'm very good at lying to myself
I live in a state of constant denial
Fry my brain with half-truths and full lies

I'm very good at lying to myself
We are just friends
You smile like that at everyone,
Holding me hostage in your pupils to the point that I don't know what color your
eyes are

I've been very good with lying to myself
You laugh like that with everyone,
Head tilted back, filling the air with your voice so that all I can hear is you
Your sly invite to dinner was given out to all of your friends
Your hands brushed theirs with the same velvet delicacy that brushed mine

I try to lie to myself more
That I am just like everyone else
There's no meaning behind your actions
They don't keep me awake at night
They don't make me look at you funny
They haven't made me start falling in love with you

And like I've said, I'm very good at lying to myself

peach rings, candy dreams
🍬🍬🍬

Sugar blows holes in my stitches
Orange-yellow rings are stuck in my throat
The almost plastic syrup cuts my vocal cords
And i cough up my words coated in blood

I don't tell him I don't want to kiss him
We turn cheeks
Bump eyelashes
I see the freckles by his ears
I will hold him together while he attempts to tether me to him

He becomes a ghost
A haunted house fugitive
His feet hit the pavement, going nowhere
I chase him down through the dial tone and harbor him in my head
The idea of him stains my nerve endings a raw red

Then he goes missing
I don't join the manhunt for a man that should've been hunted
I unpack the next set of moving boxes and find empty packages of peach rings
covering photo frames of forgotten friends

When I'm seventeen, I'll go to the corner store with my dad for a pack of cigarettes
My eyes glaze over the hundreds of candy wrappers behind the counter and my dad
wonders why I've started to cry

what can you see in the stars, really?
🐾🐾🐾

He won't let me look at his star sign
He never lets me see how his chart aligns
He thinks I'll judge him more than I already do

Which tells me he's part Scorpio
With a hint of bastard Sagittarius
His venus is in Libra so I'll never know where his heart lies
Because his heart has learned to lie on both sides of the fence
And there's gotta be a Gemini in there too
If not his Lilith, then his moon

There's too many of him
I can see each version of him
The same way I see multiple versions of him when I'm higher than I like
If anything a birthplace and time
Just confirms my suspicions

When I tell him that
He scoffs something cute about confirmation bias
Knowing he doesn't really know anything about signs,
He tosses "your Taurus is in the twentieth house" from his throat
And the confident flippancy that coats the melody of his voice
Grips my heart like a vice that forces me to let him live in his ignorance
I won't tell him I have no Taurus in my chart and that there is no such thing as a
twentieth house

I let him think he's won the banter because he smiles that stupid smile
That goofy smile
The one where we lock eyes
And he stares at me like I hung the stars, the moon, the sky
Like I created astrology
Like he knows he can't tell me what I ask him
Because I already know what I know

That his smile screams Scorpio sexuality and secrecy

His goofiness finds home with the archer
That both sides of his vulnerability but utter pride to mask it all
Has the dichotomy of twins written all over it
And because I am familiar with that smile
With that look
His Libra will balance me out
The way I already suspected it would

food for thought
🐜🐜🐜

I can't stand the taste of peas
Or cherry tomatoes
The tartness and squishy of their form is enough to make me want to vomit
everywhere
You like pasta
And so do I
When I say that you say "Pasta has tomatoes"
I want to argue about the different types of pasta until I remember that we are eating
spaghetti
And when I say we, I mean you are with your friends eating spaghetti
And I am with my friends eating the same spaghetti
You crack a joke I'm not supposed to be listening to
I crack a smile that I wish you weren't privy to
And I am just another stop on your buffet line
I allow you to take what you want from me in our bite-sized conversations
A little flirtation here
A dash of teasing there
A little too much confusion everywhere
I never thought I'd be making this relationship between you and food but nonetheless
you mention the tomatoes
I say it's all about their form
There's a moment of eye contact
Tension
Like pulling taffy that isn't gonna turn out right
But you keep pulling because getting the taffy to this point was hard as fuck
anyways
And there's no way you're gonna waste it
Then you laugh
Then I laugh
Then you're leaving
And I'm left wondering if our interactions remind you of taffy

I'm making waffles
I'm the only one in the room not nursing a hangover
Only nursing my coffee
The next thing I know you're standing next to me

Disheveled and struggling visibly but still gorgeous without trying
Like cookies melted together on a pan
I say hey because that's what you say to friends nursing hangovers
And I think you'll just wave and deal with your headache alone
But now you're staying next to me
And my waffle has 45 seconds on the clock
Your energy is weird
You compliment my outfit
It's Saturday morning brunch
And you definitely saw me in less three weekends before
Yes, the compliment was nice yet unexpected
And then pretty slips through your canines
"You're pretty" slips through your canines
It's unfamiliar
Like maple syrup on top of butter and bananas
Perfect and warm and addicting
And then you're leaving
And my waffle is beeping
I wondered if letting it burn would give you time to return but I'm not wasting food
for your soul

You sometimes remind me of a soul I did waste food on
That remembered I liked peach rings
Their sickly sweet too much for him
That he gave them to me
Even after I said I wouldn't love him on a string

I'm about to go smoke
Swap all the words in my throat
For the taste of earth in my lungs
And feel sugar in my brain for a change
I'm standing outside where your window happens to be
Waiting for my flakey ass friends
Somehow, you've found yourself outside
Roaming the edges of my vision
And I'm complaining to my friend about the puff of my hair that has yet to be proud
I say "I can't stand that it mushrooms the way it does"
And you whisper beneath your breath "I like mushrooms"

Then you're leaving again and I'm wondering
If you like mushrooms
Or my hair
Or both
Or neither and just wanted something to say to me

Either way, I take the mushrooms out of my stir fry and leave them on a plate
As if it is a summoning spell for you
As if it will make you materialize
Then I put a mushroom next to your contact name
And now I associate them with you
Which I hate
Because I never thought about mushrooms before and now that's all I do
And I never thought about you before and now that's all I do

find love for the art, find a love for the artist
❧❧❧

We leave books in the backseat

Let forlorn drafts take up space in the clouds

Leave pen ink in our footsteps

The only record we need is the one that spins on your tongue

Whispering a musical drama

A woeful retelling of nothing at all

I get caught in your grooves

As you paint me a seat in your life in my imagination

I start writing the captions in my handwriting

On your side of the page, two friends sit and share liquor, burning sweet in their stomachs,

On my side of the page, I burn my vocal cords to quietness

The silence is shared

The sentiment is selfish

My brain has written the song

Before you'd even considered a melody

I always find myself wanting to say sorry to you

As if the lack of correlation or causation that keeps causing confusion

Is my fault and my fault alone

i've missed how you taste in my imagination
♣ ♣ ♣

Chewing on gushers
A smile permanent on my face
The feeling of sour stickiness storms the palaces of my palate
Somehow, you are always akin to food

Somehow, you are always hiding in my writings
I can taste it in the letters
You are wafting from my syllables

I see you once in a blue moon
Forget that your eyes are hazel because to me they always look new
They always take me in as if I am new
As if I am all you've ever known
And all you'll ever need to know

You won't ever know how happy you make me
How you have been my unaware muse for longer than your ego would allow me to
admit
Longer than my pride would let me submit that notion to you
And we work better that way

You can't ever be mine
The idea of us intertwined across time
Is too insatiable to feed
Too hungry, too filled with hollowing greed
So I won't be upset when you leave
Or leave me with what ifs
Partially crashed on Santa Barbara cliffs
Permanently feeling like we might just kiss
If I stare at you a single second longer

my heart moves faster than my reality can check it

♣♣♣

A lot of love goes nowhere but my heart
I build cobblestone houses out of cute comments
Pave the streets with my imagination
Let the I don't knows fill in the blanks

I, a bird not freed in actuality
Only in denial
Follow the crumbs you leave between your soliloquies and slanted teeth
Down the smallest path I've ever walked
There is only one set of shoes for me to fill
But they're not the ones I want

I've realized that if I don't have what I want
I go crazy with wondering
Let my mind whisk me away to a world where I am loved by everyone I love
Where I don't lay abandoned in the snow
Watching them rush to their hearths and warm family dinners
Waiting for someone to carry my hypothermic body into their loving heart
The sun shines eternally
I am held unwaveringly
Time slows and I never wonder
Why I was picked last for love

a spiritual wake-up call for an emotional coma
🍀🍀🍀

Come back to this century, I'm calling for you
Come back to this moment, I'm calling you

The ringtone of my voice falls silent on open ears
Your body heat is cozy but your eyes are blizzards

Where are you?
Where do you go like this?
A parallel universe?
A dreamland like candyland?

I stare at you unmovingly for what is eternity
It feels like eternal connection but my side is the only one with electricity

Where have you gone?
Have you let the wind from the winding roads of sleepless nights carry you away?

A sparkler weak in light ignites behind your smile
It's mismatched with the hollow tips of empty irises

I ask you to close your eyes, rest your mind for a mile
If I were to go away in your slumber
Would I find my ears ringing me back to you?

salt and vinegar
❧ ❧ ❧

Your lip is cut and bleeding
Dripping damnation on my doorway
What do you expect me to do?
Do I look like a hospital to you?

I sit you down, with as much gentle violence as you can handle
The alcohol pads sting with my words
"Stop picking these fights"
He asks if he should pick me flowers instead
I fear for the plants' life more than his own
So I tell him to pick nothing at all
Give something of yourself for once
He says he's given me the world
I say my world is a nonviolent haven
Where I don't tend to my lover's wounds

His lip is split in two places, blistering and boiling
The blood has crusted and flakes on my couch
Metallic air fills our lungs
I lay his head in my lap
My love of our liminality weaves comfort through his hair

My lip is split in the corners
They bubble with bright red
Every time I open up to someone
With him, the wounds refuse to heal
And for once I don't want them to

He asks me if I have salt and vinegar lays
I ask if he's insane
But produce a bag from the air
We share it
The salt stings and the vinegar slaps me sappy
A boxing match we both signed up for

He asks if he can kiss me

I ask if he thinks he should heal first
He says it's the first time he doesn't want to

The vinegar of his lips pairs so softly with the salt on mine
It's painful
But damn it's good

i'm missing a tooth, i'm missing you
❧ ❧ ❧

I drown myself in memories
So I never forget what the choking feels like
I hold hands with each grim reaper
So the chill of the journey reminds me to bring a jacket when it's my time to go
I rub my tongue over where my tooth used to be
But it's not there anymore so I run my fingers over the memory of you instead
So I'll always be able to say I felt it, to say I felt you

I've locked up every thought about you
On my phone, in my brain
They are forbidden material
Banned books in the library of my psyche
That I wish I could burn to the ground

You are the worst perfect ending for me
I know that
I wish you could've been the better beginning for me
I cling to this hope, a life raft in empty sea

But hope breeds miserable maps of where we might've ended up
And I don't even know you well enough to be trapped in a car with you
Or what songs you listen to while driving
Or if you blow through red lights how you blew through me
So I keep my memory of you,
my idea of you,
untainted and partially delusional
Sealed in the folds of my cortices
At least until I see you again
And i repeat the cycle over and over and over on spiral staircases at home

the burden of remembering

❧ ❧ ❧

If I say I love you on Wednesday how you did three Tuesdays ago, will it ring a bell?
Jumpstart your psyche?
Do reruns of our run-ins start rewinding through your mind if I mention crimson collars?
Soft fabric keeping me from the cold
The cold keeping me away from you
As it rightfully should

Loving a pathological amnesiac warps your brain a special way
Your hippocampus makes space for your memories and the ones he can't seem to hold
You are a swarm of raven feathers
I carry gravel in my pockets
You are too heavy to hold in my heart
I am too flighty for you to try

When I've forcefully forgotten your birthday and you stop seeing me out of the corner of your eye
Could we ever call ourselves strangers?
Could we ever actually unknow each other?

The knowing scratches on the chalkboard of my memory
And drowns out the melody of new symphonies
When will the reminiscence of the music box tune of your voice stop haunting my room at night?
When will I be able to sleep to the rhythm of another larynx vibrating through my cranium?

I hold a memory only one of us remembers
And I always find myself wishing that the one who forgot
Was me

regretful obsession
❧ ❧ ❧

The silence of the space encased by the bubble of a bustling city was becoming
common, almost homely in a way
I had stopped looking for you around corners
in real lovers
in 18th century paintings

I stopped calling you my muse
But still write down every thought you inspire, lest I lose you in the wordplay
I never even really came close to you, don't even really know you
You, a star, a planet, Saturn spinning in the distance
Trapped me in your rings
Tossed me about in the hurricane of your questionability

You are tainted with curiosity
I don't think you give a fuck that it killed the cat because you're hoping the
satisfaction of your ego will bring it back
Are you having fun yet?
Have you got your laughs in?
Whispering about me to your roommates how I'm coiled around your finger
If you clap twice, I'll call
If you whistle, I'll wait
A social experiment turned comedy night
A pathetic puppet show
I know I've clipped my own strings but why do I still feel like I'm dancing?
Or waiting for the arrival of your footsteps to breathe life into me again

I can't ever accuse you of accosting me with your attention
I am the victim and only witness
You are judge, jury, executioner, and St. Peter's assistant rolled into a single sacred
mortal body
You've won
Truly
The only prize left is my acceptance
And lack of resistance.

abandon your muses, it's for the better
♣♣♣

I let the notes wash over me like fresh moonlight
And crashing waves
I've written them
I've sang them
I've had them sung back to me

They wash over me
A refreshing shower
After a sick night's sleep
Opening my pores
Washing away the death, the stale, the still
The cough still rings in my lungs
And in my bones

And If I listen to the wind chimes
A voice is there
I know who it is
But won't speak its name
Won't listen to it any longer
Because the melody of its tone sounds saccharine

It sounds like warm cashmere
And breezy May mornings in the sand
It's brighter than it actually was
It's sweeter than it actually is
And I'd bask in the rose-colored contact
Or I'd focus on the burning portions
And the firefighters have already put out the smoke
So I let the ashes wash over me
Let them settle into my skin
They leave me feeling chalky
Dusty
Not charred
Or destroyed
But if I think about it too long, i can feel it singeing my soul

And I let the record play
Let the same songs wash me back to godliness
I know I've missed this cleanliness
But I never knew it was missing

Songs before sound the same as songs during and songs after
Because what's after laughter
A cough
A sickness
One that I have washed off for a week but kept returning
And I found myself missing the stale
The still
the death
It's nothing another shower can't fix
And a cup of chamomile lemon tea with two honey packets
A misty morning
A night in this cute college town

I feel the voice call to me
And I do not answer

if you're reading this,
i'll never be able to thank any of you enough <3

Author's Notes

HI! Oh my god, this is my first-ever physical publication!!!! I've been writing creatively and dreaming of being a published author since I was in the second grade. I wish I could go back in time and show my second-grade self. Honestly, I didn't plan on writing this book specifically. I always thought my first publication would be a New York Times bestselling novel, definitely not a poetry book. To be honest, poetry saved my life. When I was a sophomore in high school, I was struggling mentally and the newly established poetry club offered me the perfect outlet. I just never expected it to become my life's purpose. This book follows an insane crush I had on the worst person you could ever have a crush on. Luckily, I'm done with that but I have to give this person credit where credit is due. Without them, I wouldn't have written such beautiful, heart-wrenching poetry and I definitely wouldn't be releasing this book. So, dude, if you ever read this (which even if you did, you wouldn't realize it was about you until sixty years down the line) thank you? I think? I guess? Anyway, an actual huge thank you if you read this far, because this was the hardest thing I've ever done. I hate perception and always believe my work can be 10 times better than it currently is. Thank you, I love you, and find love in unorthodox places! (that isn't illegal of course!) <3

-Khayan (like the pepper)

P.S: l actually can't stand peach rings now lol

.

P.S: l actually can't stand peach rings now lol

Made in the USA
Las Vegas, NV
17 December 2023